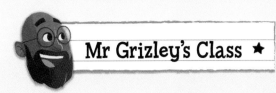

Mr Grizley's Class ★

Camila's PLAN

by Bryan Patrick Avery   illustrated by Arief Putra

raintree

a Capstone company — publishers for childre

T0372068

Raintree is an imprint of Capstone Global Library Limited,
a company incorporated in England and Wales having its
registered office at 264 Banbury Road, Oxford, OX2 7DY –
Registered company number: 6695582

www.raintree.co.uk
myorders@raintree.co.uk

Designed by Dina Her
Original illustrations © Capstone Global Library Limited 2024
Originated by Capstone Global Library Ltd
Printed and bound in India

978 1 3982 5278 3

British Library Cataloguing in Publication Data
A full catalogue record for this book is available from the
British Library.

CONTENTS

Mr Grizley's Class ★

Cecilia Gomez

Shaw Quinn

Emily Kim

Mordecai Foster

Nathan Wu

Ashok Aparnam

Ryan Clayborn

Rahma Abdi

Nicole Washington

Alijah Wilson

Suddha Agarwal

Chad Werner

Semira Madani

Pierre Boucher

Zoe Charmichael

Dmitry Orloff

Camila Jennings

Madison Tanaka

Annie Barberra

Bobby Lewis

CHAPTER 1

Votes

Camila sat at her desk and doodled in her notebook.

"Camila," Shaw said, "who did you pick for school council?"

Camila shrugged. "Isn't that supposed to be secret?" she asked.

Shaw looked around, then whispered.

"I voted for you," he said.

"Me?" Camila asked.

Mordecai leaned towards Camila. "I voted for you too," he said.

Shaw nodded. "So did Pierre and Ryan," he said.

"Why would you vote for me?"
Camila asked.

Before Shaw could answer,
Mr Grizley stood up from his desk.
"I've tallied the votes," he said.

"Who won?" Annie called out.

Mr Grizley smiled.

"Drum roll, please," he said.

The class drummed on their desks. They drummed faster and faster until Mr Grizley put up his hand for quiet. The room went silent.

"Your new school council representative is . . . Camila!"

The class cheered. Everyone except Camila.

Camila sat at her desk and looked around at her classmates. "Why me?" she wondered.

CHAPTER 2

Plans

At break time, Camila played catch with Annie and Madison.

"What are you going to do on the school council?" Annie asked.

"I don't really have a plan," Camila said.

"Well, you could make me ball monitor," Madison said. She held up their ball. "Dmitry always gives the good balls to the boys."

"We get the old, flat balls," Annie agreed.

"Okay," Camila said. "Madison can be our new ball monitor."

"I'll go and let Dmitry know," Madison said as she skipped away.

"Can I be the eco-leader?" Annie asked.

Camila thought for a moment.

"I suppose Ashok has been doing it for a long time," she said. "Yes, you can take over."

"I'll go and tell everyone," Annie said.

"Being on the school council is easy," Camila thought.

Back inside, Dmitry stopped at Camila's desk.

"You replaced me?" he asked.

"Um . . . yes," Camila said.

"That's not fair!" Dmitry said.

"She replaced me too," Ashok said. "I can't believe it."

Camila sighed. Maybe being on the school council wasn't so easy after all.

"Okay, Dmitry, you can still be ball monitor," Camila said. "Ashok can be eco-leader."

"You told me that I could be eco-leader," Annie said.

"And I'm supposed to be ball monitor," Madison said.

The whole class gathered around Camila's desk. It seemed like everyone was cross with her. Camila closed her eyes and covered her ears.

CHAPTER 3

Leadership

Mr Grizley rang a bell on his desk. The children returned to their seats.

Mr Grizley took Camila out to the corridor to talk.

"I don't think I can be on the school council," she said.

"It's hard," Mr Grizley said. "That doesn't mean you can't do it."

Camila sighed. "I don't know what everyone wants me to do," she said.

"Well, what do *you* want to do?" Mr Grizley asked.

"I've got an idea," Camila said. "But I don't know if I can do it."

"You can if you think you can," Mr Grizley said.

"Maybe you're right," Camila said. Then, she smiled. "I can do it!"

Camila returned to the classroom.

"I'm sorry for the trouble I've caused today," she told the class. "But I've got an idea, and I'm going to need some help."

The class listened.

"But first," Camila said, "Dmitry and Madison will work together as ball monitors. That way, everyone gets a fair chance at using the best balls."

Dmitry and Madison nodded.

"Annie and Ashok can take turns as eco-leader," Camila said. "Is that fair?"

"Perfect," they said.

Camila looked at her class.

"I want our class to lead a recycling scheme for the school," she said. "I'll need volunteers to help plan. I'll also need help going to other classrooms. Do any of you want to help?"

Every hand went up.

"That sounds great!" Annie said.

"I'd love to help," Dmitry said.

"You're going to make a great representative," Mr Grizley said.

"Thanks to all of you," Camila said, "I just might."

LET'S MAKE A SELF-TALK SUPERHERO

In the story, Camila learned to stop telling herself she couldn't be a good leader. When she told herself that she could do it, her whole attitude changed. Camila's positive self-talk helped give her confidence. Positive self-talk can be a superpower that will help you accomplish more than you ever thought possible. We're going to create our own Self-talk Superhero to help remind us of the power of positive self-talk.

WHAT YOU NEED:

- white or coloured paper
- coloured pens, pencils or crayons
- scissors (optional)

WHAT TO DO:

1. Draw your Self-talk Superhero on the paper. Your hero can be whatever or whoever you want. Be creative!

2. Colour in your hero. Use as many or as few colours as you would like.

3. (Optional) Cut out your hero. If you'd rather keep your paper the way it is, that's okay too.

4. Give your hero a name and write it on the back of the picture.

Keep your Self-talk Superhero close by. You can carry it in your school bag or put it up on your wall. Your Self-talk Superhero will be a great reminder that you can do anything if you believe in yourself. That's the power of positive self-talk!

GLOSSARY

doodle draw small designs or scribbles

gather come together around something

monitor pupil who is asked to help a teacher with a certain job

recycling process of treating used or waste materials so they can be reused

replace put something new in place

tally count

whisper speak very softly

After reading

Apply learning: Discuss the book. Ask: *Were you surprised by the end of the story? Why or why not?*

Comprehension

- Where was Clare playing? (under the pear tree)
- Who was in the bear costume? (Miss Windermere)
- What were Mum and Dad going to do with the bear? (snare it with a net)

Fluency

- Pick a page that most of the group read quite easily. Ask them to reread it with pace and expression. Model how to do this if necessary.
- In pairs, children can read the dialogue on page 10, reading for either Mum or Dad. Encourage them to make it sound as though the characters are really talking, paying attention to exclamation and question marks.
- Practise reading the words on page 17.

Tricky words review

someone	oh	ask
says	our	some
friend	laugh	have
doing	what	today
once	water	were

TALK ABOUT IT

1. Camila was surprised that her classmates chose her to be on the school council. Why do you think that was?

2. Annie and Madison gave Camila advice on what to do on the school council. Do you think they were helpful? Why or why not?

3. Camila replaced Dmitry as ball monitor and Ashok as eco-leader. Do you think that was fair? Why or why not?

WRITE ABOUT IT

1. What would you want to do if you were on your school council? Make a list with three or more things.

2. Do you think that Camila will go on to be a good leader? Write a paragraph explaining your answer.

3. Pretend you are Camila and write a speech about the recycling scheme that you can share with other classes.

ABOUT THE AUTHOR

Bryan Patrick Avery discovered his love of reading and writing at an early age when he received his first Bobbsey Twins mystery. He writes picture books, chapter books and graphic novels. He is the author of the picture book *The Freeman Field Photograph*, as well as "The Magic Day Mystery" in *Super Puzzletastic Mysteries*. Bryan lives in northern California, USA, with his family.

ABOUT THE ILLUSTRATOR

Arief Putra loves working and drawing in his home studio at the corner of Yogyakarta city in Indonesia. He enjoys coffee, cooking, space documentaries and solving the Rubik's Cube. Living in a small house in a rural area with his wife and two sons, Arief has a big dream to spread positivity around the world through his art.